Secrets and Senet

To Hythe Primary

I hope this inspires your love of reading and ancient history!

T.F.Taylor

T. FREYA TAYLOR

ILLUSTRATED BY - JAMES KOENIG

The Mummy's Curse: Secrets and Senet

By T. Freya Taylor, Illustrated by James Koenig

Illustrations by James Koenig - www.freelancefridge.com

ISBN 979-8-753-93797-1

freyat933@gmail.com

To my parents, partner and original 4T class who were the motivation and inspiration to write and publish this story.

To my godson Oliver-James, who is fascinated with archaeology and history, may this inspire you to keep following your dreams.

Finally, to my dear friend Cat, may you forever walk peacefully and blissfully in the field of reeds.

- T. Freya Taylor -

To my grandparents, who cultivated my artistic endeavors as well as my interest in Egyptian culture.

- James Koenig -

Contents

Chapter 1 – Friendly Competition.....................1

Chapter 2 – Exploring in the Shadows.................9

Chapter 3 – Unexpected Friends........................17

Chapter 4 – Khemu's Wisdom..........................39

Chapter 5 – Payback time...............................47

Glossary – 58

How to Play Senet – 63

Hieroglyphic Alphabet and Numbers –..............67

The Mummy's Curse

Chapter 1

Friendly Competition

One afternoon, after walking for hours in the blistering heat of the Egyptian sun, best friends Thoth and Ammon's eyes landed upon a familiar sight.

Emerging from the golden sands, stood the remains of an ancient palace which had always stood guard over their village. Unsurprisingly, many stories had been passed down over the generations about this mysterious place, but the boys believed they were the only ones alive who were brave enough to step foot inside the towering palace walls. No one else had any reason to come this far away from the main trade routes and the safety of the village… unless you were seeking an adventure.

Before long, the boys entered the grand entranceway which was flanked by once majestic statues of a forgotten pharaoh. However, the facial features, that would have helped to identify him, had long eroded away. Passing through the tall, intricately carved columns, the friends decided to take shelter from the

sun in their usual spot; pausing momentarily to take a sip of the now warm liquid from their waterskins.

"Shall we?" Ammon asked his friend, while retrieving their senet game board out of the drawstring bag that hung around his waist. Game in hand, he settled cross-legged on the cool sand.

"Only if you promise not to cheat this time." The younger boy, Thoth, replied. Taking a seat on the opposite side of a fallen stone pillar, he continued, "I know you're two years older than me, but it doesn't mean you get to win every time."

With a roll of his eyes, Ammon opened the hidden draw in the senet box (which held the games pieces and throwing sticks) and carefully placed each piece on their starting positions. After half an hour, it was clear Thoth was losing… terribly.

"It's not fair, you're cheating! You've made a barricade against my pieces!" He huffed, folding his arms over his bare chest and pouting.

"I am not!" declared the older boy, laughing at his best friend's reaction. "I'm clearly just better at throwing sticks than you. The more sticks that land coloured side up, means you get to move more spaces. They're the rules Thoth, I'm winning fair and square."

"But I never get more than two or three each turn, I might as well give up. I've got no more moves left." Thoth replied miserably, "We've been playing for years and I'm still no good at it, Ammon."

Thoth then reached up to twirl a few strands of thick, dark hair from his plaited side-lock (which was the sign he was still young in the eyes of Egyptian society) around his right index finger.

"Thoth, you are named after the god of wisdom himself! Your parents wouldn't have named you that if you weren't capable of achieving great things. That includes winning a game of senet." Ammon sincerely assured him, then extended his right hand to help Thoth to his feet. "Although, you should probably think about changing your name to Khonsu. Even a god can lose dreadfully at senet!"

At this, Thoth let himself fall back into the sand and his head fell straight into his hands.

"I haven't lost five days of moonlight just yet, only about a million games of senet." He moaned pitifully. "Can we see who can get the best of three games?"

"I'd love to, but I think we'd still be here well after Ra's sun barque has passed into the underworld," Ammon laughed. "However, all is not lost my friend. My brother Adjo is fishing in the Nile and has promised a great feast for tonight."

He held out his hand for a second time and Thoth finally made it to his feet. As soon as the game board was safely tucked back into the drawstring bag, they started the long walk back home to their village.

In the distance, lanterns were starting to spring up in windows and doorways, signalling the start of the evening. As the two boys became small figures in the ever-shifting sands, they didn't notice a small pair of eyes that were peeking out from behind one of the columns, watching them both with curiosity.

Chapter 2

Exploring in the shadows

A couple of days after their last game of senet, Thoth and Ammon returned to their hideout to practise once again. They preferred it here as the air wasn't as humid as it was in the village and they could shelter in the shadows of the beautifully carved stone walls.

Today they decided to settle beneath an intricately carved quartz statue of a Pharaoh. Even though Thoth couldn't read hieroglyphs, he studied the monument more closely and could just make out the cartouche, which held this great ruler's name in hieroglyphs, even though it was partially covered by the golden sand.

Looking up, he saw Ammon gesturing for him to hurry up and start a new game. It was clear the time apart had done wonders for Thoth's confidence; as Ammon was pleasantly surprised at how well he was playing today. He'd even managed to overtake a couple of Ammon's own game pieces!

Not wanting his younger friend to win just yet, he thought of a new tactic.

"You know, Set was telling me this place is haunted." Ammon announced during Thoth's next turn. Looking up, he saw the younger boy's eyes widen in panic. He had frozen mid-move and his senet piece was dangerously close to dropping into the sand. Ammon then rustled his shoulder-length, dark hair and nonchalantly smoothed down his white, linen tunic. His lips turned up slightly in a smile as his plan was clearly working.

"H-Haunted? By what??" He uttered, his eyes darting around the palace as if expecting to see something in the shadows.

"Some say it's the gods coming down to watch over how the mortals are treating the world they created. But others say it's mummies that lurk within the shadows of their resting places." Ammon smiled slyly, knowing his best friend was scared of mummies coming back to life.

"Mummies? But… th-they don't come back to life. They can't! That's why we mummify people, so they can live forever in the afterlife, not come back to life on Earth, right?" Thoth asked shakily.

"Maybe. I mean, that's what the elders and the scriptures tell us, but who really knows? There has always been talk of a 'mummy's curse' hasn't there?" Ammon whispered, as he sneakily moved ahead of Thoth's piece.

Suddenly, the younger boy's body shivered as the hot desert air turned eerily cold around him.

"Ammon? Did you feel that?" he whispered, not daring to move a muscle.

"Feel what?" The older boy replied, not bothering to

look up from calculating where his wooden game piece could go next.

"I just felt…" Thoth began, but immediately stopped, as his chocolate brown eyes connected to another set of glinting orbs in the shadows.

"AMMON! LOOK OVER THERE!" he shouted, fear taking over his body.

Immediately, he jumped back and darted to hide behind the statue he'd been sitting under, but in doing so, he had knocked the gameboard over and sent it, and the ten playing pieces, flying into the sand.

"Thoth!" Ammon groaned, "In the name of the gods, why did you do that? All because you were losing? You really do need to grow up. I'm going home, I've had enough of this." As he turned to leave, Thoth tugged on his arm to stop him.

"I swear to Ra, I didn't knock it over on purpose. I saw something over there in the shadows, I promise Ammon!" Thoth quietly pleaded with his best friend, pointing behind him where he thought he saw a pair of eyes.

"Whatever Thoth, I'll see you tomorrow." Ammon muttered, leaving the senet board and game pieces behind as he walked away, his shoulders slouched and his hands balled into fists. Usually, Ammon never let the game board out of his sight so the fact he had left it without a second glance, worried Thoth that his friendship might be in trouble.

Suddenly, Thoth felt scared, frustrated and alone, but he did know one thing for certain. He had to find out who those eyes belonged to. If nothing else, to prove to Ammon he was not a liar.

Chapter 3

Unexpected Friends

Determined (and still a little bit scared), Thoth stepped out from his hiding place and ventured towards the inner courtyard which was further than they had ever explored before.

Moving through the shadows of the palace, he scanned the floor for something he could set alight to guide his way. Luckily, he saw a piece of cloth lying half-covered in the sand. He quickly wrapped it around a torch handle that had still been in its bracket on the wall and struck a rock to create a spark. Gripping the blazing torch tightly in his left hand, he began his search. Clinging to a small amount of hope that he could find some clues as to who else was there with him in this forgotten place.

After what felt like an eternity, Thoth took a deep breath and sat down on the sand covered stone floor. Feeling disheartened that he was no further forward in his quest for the truth. Taking a moment, he held the torch higher to the wall of the corridor, until he could clearly make out the intricate carvings. In the middle of the space, a Pharaoh sat upon a grand throne. Thoth assumed the lady standing next to him on his right-hand side was the queen. Interestingly, there were also two children sat playing senet at their feet! On the king's other side, was a young man wearing a solemn expression. Thoth noticed he was wearing a kilt and the striped nemes headdress, which was usually worn only by the Pharaohs.

He must be the crown prince! Thoth thought, wishing once more he could read the name within the royal cartouche. Maybe this family called this palace home?

As Thoth continued to hold his torchlight higher, above their depictions he could see yellow stars carved onto the ceiling, that seemed to dance in the torchlight. Their vivid colour stood out boldly against the azure blue background which mimicked the night sky. Thoth remembered what Ammon's brother Adjo had once told him, that sailors (like him) used the stars to find their way home. Silently, Thoth took a moment to pray to the gods, hoping that he too could find what he was looking for.

Then he heard it.

Laughter.

Coming from somewhere up ahead.

Curiously, Thoth tiptoed toward the unusually happy sound echoing through the chamber. Strangely, Thoth didn't feel frightened by the sound but comforted by it instead. As he got closer, Thoth hoped he would find out if the owner of the eyes he had been searching for, was also the source of the laughter.

As he turned the corner, Thoth was astounded at the sight that greeted him.

The laughter was coming from a small mummy!

The young boy had to blink a couple of times just to make sure he wasn't imagining anything; as not only was the small mummy kneeling on the floor of the chamber in front of him, but Thoth couldn't believe the reason he was laughing. Next to him, he was excitedly watching TWO MORE - slightly taller - mummies playing a game of senet on a board that looked very familiar.

Finding his courage, Thoth cleared his throat and took a large step forward into the cavernous, well-lit chamber.

"Excuse me, but I think that's mine."

Immediately, the three mummies stopped, turned and stared agape at the young Egyptian boy.

"Can you see us?" asked the small, kneeling mummy who had laughed earlier. Thoth thought he couldn't have been older than seven, as he had to stretch himself up tall to see who had spoken.

"Of course I can, you're real aren't you?" Thoth replied, "and by the looks of it, you're a lot better at senet than I am." He pointed at the game the tallest mummy was currently winning.

"Well, we have been playing for over a thousand years." The older mummy, who looked to be about sixteen, replied with a sad smile and shrugged his shoulders. Tutting, as he adjusted his bandages that had slipped slightly with the gesture.

"I'm Thoth." The not-so nervous boy stated, stretching out his hand for the mummies to shake.

"Would you like us to teach you how to play, Thoth?" the smallest mummy squeaked, as he eagerly got to his feet to shake the boy's hand. His familiar, dark eyes glinting in the torchlight.

“Don’t be rude Djedefre, he knows how to play the game, everyone does. It's been around for longer than we have.” The female mummy, who looked to be around twelve, replied matter-of-factly, as she too stood up from the golden stool she was sitting on, to shake his hand. The beautifully coloured beads in her hair twinkling with every movement.

"But Nefertiabet! He has just said he needed to practice, we can help him!" The youngest mummy then folded his arms over his chest before muttering, "and you know I like being called Djed."

"And you know I prefer being called Nefer!" His older sister snapped back and they began to bicker furiously causing Thoth to laugh. Instantly, they reminded him of how Ammon and his brother Adjo would bicker with their sister Yuya over the smallest of things. A small pang in Thoth's stomach at the memory of how Ammon left him alone, only spurred Thoth on to find out more about why these three mummies were here.

"Thoth," the tallest mummy interrupted loudly, finally getting to his feet from a slightly larger and even more beautifully gilded chair. "It's very nice to meet you." He was the last to shake Thoth's hand before putting gently resting a hand on each of his siblings' shoulders, which caused them to stop arguing immediately.

"Would you like to play a game of senet with my brother, sister and I?"

"I'd love that!" Thoth replied eagerly, "Maybe you can teach me how to beat my friend Ammon? He always wins when we play together." Thoth admitted, taking a seat at the older mummy's indication beside his three new friends.

"Don't worry Thoth," Djed squeaked, "my big brother Kawab Khufu is the best senet player ever!"

"Khufu? Didn't you build the Great Pyramid of Giza?"

Thoth asked in surprise, "I thought you'd be older."

"Sorry to disappoint," the older mummy replied, "Khufu would be our father, so I prefer to go by Kawab. I take it he completed his great structure, then? I only got to see a few years of it before… well, before I ended up here." Kawab admitted, with a hint of sadness in his voice, "anyway, let's teach you how to win this timeless game." The older mummy continued, avoiding the subject of how the three mummies found themselves in the grand palace.

Thoth didn't want to ask why his new friends weren't resting peacefully in the afterlife just yet, as he assumed it would be a subject best left for when they knew each other better.

The three mummies and Thoth then spent the next few hours practising tactics and enjoying each other's company. It was only as Thoth noticed his torchlight had been extinguished and there was only a faint glow of the embers coming from the flames in the mummies' chamber, did he think it was probably time to go home.

"Kawab, Nefer and Djed, how can I ever thank you for today? I've learned so many senet tactics I can't wait to use with Ammon! How can I ever repay you?" Thoth asked sincerely. He was disappointed he had to leave, especially as he didn't want his friends to be alone in the dark palace.

"Could we maybe keep the senet board?" Djed asked sweetly, looking up to Thoth, "please?" He added quickly after a raised eyebrow from his older brother.

“Djed!” Nefer immediately scolded her younger sibling, “we can’t ask for something that isn’t ours. Besides, we have lots of senet boards and other games in our room.”

“But they aren’t real, Nefer! The pieces are stuck to the board or locked in the drawers so we can’t play.” Djed cried.

Thoth noticed a small tear had trickled down the young mummy’s face and he realised just how much playing this game had meant to him. “Why are they stuck to the board? That doesn’t make any sense.” Thoth asked curiously.

“Would you like to see what we mean?” Kawab asked, “It might be easier to understand that way.”

The oldest mummy held out his arm for Thoth to take, and as he did so, Thoth felt a strange weightlessness in the pit of his stomach. He took a moment to open his eyes and for the second time today, he couldn't believe what he saw.

Kawab, Nefer, Djed and Thoth were all standing in the middle of a grand chamber. It was filled with the finest, golden and intricately carved items Thoth had ever seen! It was almost as though he had been transported into the middle of a legendary story like Khemu, the village elder, had told him when he was younger. A tale of a great pharaoh who had treasure beyond all comprehension. Maybe Khemu knew about this place and used it for inspiration for his stories? Or maybe Khemu's stories were real?

"This is our room!" Djed squeaked excitedly, bringing

Thoth back from his thoughts, as he showed him around the chamber, "This is my bed, that's Nefer's and that big one in the corner is Kawab's!"

The small mummy pointed to each sarcophagus in turn. All three were painted beautifully and made of glinting, solid gold. The cartouches carved upon them, reminded Thoth of ones he had seen earlier on the walls of the palace.

Quickly, Djed had moved from the sarcophagi over to a small antechamber which held all of their offerings for their journey to the afterlife. Amongst the furniture, food and small shabti statues, were a vast array of games. All of them had indeed been made of elaborately carved wood, ivory or beautiful blue faience but none of them had pieces that were accessible. The senet boxes in particular had drawers that had been sealed shut or the pieces were carved into the board itself.

Playing these games is impossible, Thoth thought as he handled one of the boxes.

“Our parents thought it would be a symbol of the games for us to play in the afterlife.

Senet, Mehen, Hounds and Jackals, you name it, they're all here. They never thought we'd need to play with them in this world." Nefer told Thoth, watching his frustration as he tried to pry open the small drawers.

"I'm sorry if this sounds rude,," Thoth started, "but, why aren't you all in the afterlife? That's what we believe, isn't it? As soon as your spirit leaves your body you enter the underworld and live peacefully for eternity. Why can't you do that?" He asked thoughtfully, hoping he hadn't upset his new friends.

The three mummies looked solemn for a moment, before Kawab spoke softly.

"Well Thoth, we were all taken from this world earlier than we were meant to depart it. When we passed into the underworld, we were welcomed by Osiris himself. As god of the afterlife, he believed it would be wrong to separate us from this world for eternity because we were so young. We didn't have much of a chance to live our Earthly lives."

Thoth was stunned at this admission and nodded for Kawab to continue.

"Therefore, two days a week, our ka and our ba reunite with our human form. This allows us to wake into our human bodies and play in the palace we once called home, for as long as we like."

"Wow, the gods really are merciful." Thoth managed to utter, still in shock that the gods he had worshipped all of his life were definitely real! Suddenly, a brilliant idea popped into Thoth's mind.

"Well, as we are all now friends. I would be honoured if you would let me come and play senet with you for as long as I can?"

"You'd really do that, Thoth?" Nefer asked in surprise, no one had ever wanted to speak with them before, let alone be their friend and play their favourite game.

"Of course, I will! But first, will you help me play a prank on Ammon? He deserves something after leaving me here all alone! Well, before I met you three of course."

Three sets of eyes gleamed mischievously. Then, they

agreed the two boys would return to the palace next week for Thoth's perfect revenge prank.

Chapter 4

Khemu's Wisdom

That evening when Thoth had returned to the village, he had found Ammon by the river fishing with his brother. Slowly, the younger boy had approached the brothers and apologised to his friend for the way he had acted earlier. He blamed the fact he was a bit scared of the story Ammon had told him and used that as an excuse to get out of losing the game. Ammon forgave him without a second thought and agreed to return the following week for a rematch.

For the next couple of days, Thoth couldn't think of

anything else apart from his new friends; he was determined to know everything he could about them. On the fourth day after meeting Kawab, Djed and Nefer, Thoth decided to pay a visit to the village elder Khemu; who lived in a small hut at the top of the village, to see if he knew anything more. Nervously, Thoth waited by the doorway and saw the older gentleman sitting by his fire, roasting a piece of meat for his supper.

"Excuse me, Khemu, sir, do you know anything of the ancient palace in the desert?"

The older man looked up, surprised at seeing someone so young at his door. Usually it was adults complaining about problems in the town.

"Ah young Thoth, come in and take a seat." The older man replied, gesturing to the seat next to him.

Thoth timidly sat down and waited patiently for the old man to speak again. "The palace in the desert has stood watch over our village for over one thousand years and you're the first one to talk about it so openly in maybe 500 of them."

"But why doesn't anyone mention it? It's so grand and beautiful!" Thoth couldn't help but wonder out loud. "I remember being told stories about a grand palace when I was younger. Is it the same palace, Khemu?"

"Well, young Thoth, people like to talk about the old ways and the grandeur of the Pharaohs. Always thinking back to a 'better time'. However, that palace has always stood to the south of our village, hidden in the shadow of the sands. People know it is there, but they do not discuss it. They believe it is haunted. That it is cursed by the spirits of those who should be walking in the field of reeds, instead of walking through the shadows of the palace." The older man's eyes gleamed in the firelight as he turned to look at the curious youngster.

So the story was true.

Wonder and excitement started to course through Thoth's body at the thought.

"But, sir, do you know who lived there? Why would they haunt the palace? Surely the field of reeds is where we all end up after death? That's what we all want and prepare for throughout our lives."

Khemu inhaled deeply, "their names have been lost to the sands of time. However, I'm sure if someone, who knew how to read hieroglyphs, visited the site; they might be able to bring them alive once again."

"But who would be willing to go? If everyone thinks it's haunted?" the young boy asked his elder, "What if the story is lost forever?"

"Thoth, you are named after the god of wisdom and wise men know when to stop searching for answers. If you are meant to find out the story of the palace, then you will do so, I have no doubt."

A silence filled the air in Khemu's hut which Thoth took it as his cue to leave . As he stood, he heard Khemu speak once more.

"Be careful Thoth. Remember, the sands can grant your wishes, or it can take them away just as quickly."

The young boy nodded and walked slowly back to his own family's hut. That night he lay wide awake, pondering over the words Khemu had spoken to him. Was it really his destiny to bring Kawab's family's story back to life? He just had to wait and see.

Chapter 5

Payback Time

Exactly one week later, the two boys returned to the palace in the desert and set up their senet board on the same fallen pillar. Ammon was the one to speak first.

"I thought you were too scared to come back here."

"I was at first," Thoth replied honestly, "but just like you told me, I need to be braver and not give up so easily. I want to win a game because I've earned it. So here we are, in the presence of the gods, playing with no distractions."

"I like this new attitude of yours," Ammon replied, impressed his best friend seemed to have matured within the last week, "so what do I win when I beat you then?" he smirked, as he rolled a six and moved past all of Thoth's playing pieces. Before Thoth could reply, Ammon's face went very pale as he noticed something moving in the shadows.

"Thoth, there's something over there." He whispered and pointed to the dark area behind Thoth, wanting him to turn around and see for himself.

"No there isn't Ammon. Remember, it's just your imagination," Thoth replied calmly, trying to keep a neutral face, "just focus on the game. You're almost losing!"

"Thoth, I swear to the gods Nut and Geb, there is something there!" Ammon insisted, his voice shaking. Suddenly, he heard movement in front of him and looked down at the senet board. Much to his surprise, he could see the pieces moving perfectly from square to square, seemingly by themselves.

"What's happening?" Ammon shrieked, gesturing at the board, not understanding why Thoth was still sitting there laughing when this place was clearly haunted!

"Forget this Thoth! I'm not coming back here ever again, there IS a curse! I knew it!"

Without a second glance, Ammon ran as fast as he could out of the palace walls and back towards their village. As soon as he got there, he told anyone who would listen all about the real mummy's curse that had come to life in the abandoned palace. However, everyone laughed and took no notice of him. They were accustomed to Ammon playing pranks and they thought this was just his most elaborate one yet.

Back at the palace, Thoth took a few deep breaths to

help control his laughter after seeing his best friend running away from 'the spirits' that were haunting him. It wasn't something he would let his friend forget anytime soon. Thoth hoped he would remember this feeling the next time Ammon decided to play a prank on anyone. The young boy looked down at the game board and started to pick up the pieces that had fallen, when a small voice broke through the silence.

"Will he come back?" Djed asked out loud, as he stepped out of the shadows and pulled on Thoth's tunic to get his attention. "It's nice having more friends to play with."

"Maybe one day Djed," Thoth shrugged, "but we'll let him think there really is a mummy's curse for just a little bit longer. Then I'll introduce you properly."

With a smile, Thoth picked up the final piece, closed the small drawer under the game board for the final time and handed it over to Djed. The grateful smile on his new friend's face was worth every time the game had been interrupted or scattered into the sand. This game would bind them together for eternity.

The four new friends spent the rest of the afternoon playing within the palace walls, causing laughter and joy

to fill the corridors once more. In the courtyard, Thoth watched as Kawab leaned against a statue and he suddenly realised the statue of the pharaoh they had played senet under, was a true likeness of his new friends' father. Pharaoh Khufu.

It was fate! Thoth thought, that he had met his three new friends through sitting under this very statue.

That evening, Thoth waved goodbye to his friends and promised to return on their next waking day. The three mummies yawned loudly as they returned to their sarcophagi once more, feeling content they had had one of the best days in a long time.

Kawab tucked in his younger siblings before finally climbing back into his own resting place. After saying a quick prayer of thanks to the gods for their new friend Thoth, all three mummies closed their eyes and slept peacefully, for the first time in over one thousand years.

Close by, in a small, remote village in ancient Egypt. A young boy named Thoth was lying in his own bed, thinking of how much he wanted to tell the story of his new best friends. He had already planned to go and find Khemu first thing in the morning and ask to be taught how to read and write hieroglyphs. Kawab, Nefer and Djed were once lost to the sands of time, but Thoth would make sure everyone in his village and the surrounding areas knew their names once more.

Everyone must know how important they were.

Everyone must know it was their mastaba that was

carved into the hillside.

Everyone must know Pharaoh Khufu's legacy is still alive in the desert sands.

Thoth repeated this mantra to himself until he fell fast asleep, dreaming of the day he could help his new friends live forever. Thoth knew it was his destiny to make sure they were never forgotten again.

So take a moment now to say their names.

Kawab,

Nefertiabet,

Djedefre.

May you live for eternity in the field of reeds.

The End.

Glossary

Senet – a board game played by the ancient Egyptians. Its full name is 'senet net hab' which means the 'game of passing through'. This is because the aim of the game is to get from one end of the board to the other. Some historians believe it is the forerunner of backgammon and even Tutankhamun was buried with 4 different boards! See the context page to find the rules for the game so you can play yourself.

Waterskin – A container used for carrying water, usually made from the bladder of a sheep.

Thoth – was the ancient Egyptian god of writing, magic, wisdom and the moon. Thoth is usually por trayed with the body of a man but the head of an ibis or baboon.

Ammon – Another name for the Egyptian god Amun who was the god of sun and air. He also represented 'hiddenness' or 'obscurity'.

Khonsu – was the god of the moon and loved to gamble. He once lost 5 days of moonlight to the goddess Nut in a game of senet. Khonsu is sometimes shown with the head of hawk, but more often is shown as a young man with a side-lock of hair like an Egyptian youth.

Kawab, Nefertiabet and Djedefre – were three of the real children of Khufu who famously built the Great Pyramid of Giza. Kawab was the crowned prince of Egypt and would have taken over the throne if he hadn't passed away before his father. Djedefre also took over the throne of Egypt, but died without a male heir. The throne then passed onto his other famous brother Khafre who built the second tallest pyramid at the Giza plateau. Nefertiabet was Khufu's eldest daughter. All of his children were buried in a mastaba tomb near the Great Pyramid of Giza.

Ra – The god of Kings, the Sun, order and the sky. The ancient Egyptians believed it was Ra that would steer his solar barque (similar to a boat) across the sky, allowing the Sun to move across the sky during the day. At night, it was believed Ra would descend into the underworld and fight off different monsters; in order to be born again at daybreak.

Mastaba – Is a type of Egyptian tomb that was rectangular in shape. It had angled sides like a pyramid but had a flat roof instead, usually made from mud-brick or carved into a hill-side.

Cartouche – An oval-shaped frame which would surround the hieroglyphs that represent the name of a royal person or a god. The best example of this is the Abydos King List found at the Temple of Seti I at Abydos.

Ka – A person's life force that would separate from the body after death. The reason the Egyptians believed the sarcophagus and death mask had to resemble the deceased was so the Ka could recognise the body when it returned each night.

Ba – Another spiritual entity, the Ba would take the shape of a bird and had the power to travel between the worlds of the living and the dead.

Nut and Geb – Nut was the goddess of the sky and Geb was the god of the Earth.

Nemes Headdress – This is a striped, cloth headdress worn by Pharaohs and sometimes the Crowned Prince in Ancient Egypt. It covered the whole head and the nape of the neck and also had two decorative flaps (called lappets) coming down behind the ears to rest in front of the shoulders. It was considered a symbol of royalty and can be seen on many statues, carvings and papyri. The most famous example of a Nemes headdress is on the deathmask of King Tutankhamun.

How to Play Senet:

What you'll need:

- A senet board

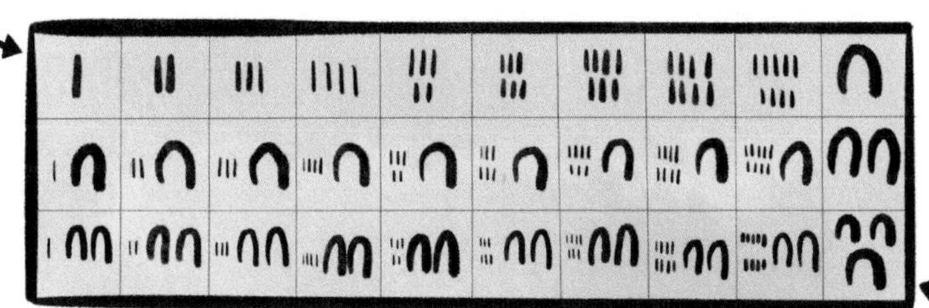

- 10 playing pieces (5 for each player) called spools and cones (you can make these or use counters too).

- 4 Throw sticks (you can use lollipop sticks with one side coloured in) or a dice.

How to use throw sticks:

- You get to move one space for every stick that lands coloured side up.
- If you throw all uncoloured sides up, you get to move 5 spaces. If you're using a dice, ignore any rolls of 6 and just roll the dice again.

Rules of the game:

1. Place all of the playing pieces on the 1-10 squares on the board. Alternating between spools and cones.
2. Both players roll/ throw the sticks and whoever gets the highest score moves first.
3. Move your first piece according to how many the dice or throw sticks show.

4. Only one piece can be on any square at one time and you must move a different piece with each turn.
5. You can jump over another player's piece, but you can't occupy a space that your piece is already on.
6. You can however swap another player's piece for yours if you land on their space.
7. Pieces can't be swapped if they're next to a piece that's the same. However, three of the same pieces in a row can form a 'blockade' which can't be jumped over or swapped. (You can jump over your own blockade).
8. You must make a move if you can.
9. If not, then you've got to pass your turn.
10. Finally, the first player to get all of their pieces off the board, wins!

Special squares:

- Square 15 – is called the 'House of Life' and is a safe square. No pieces can be swapped from this square.

- Square 26 – you must land on this square in order to complete the game. For example, if you land on square 25, you must roll a one until you move onto this square.

- Squares 26-30 – Players can leave the board from any of these squares depending on the amount of throwing sticks/number shown on the dice.

Hieroglyphic Alphabet and Numbers

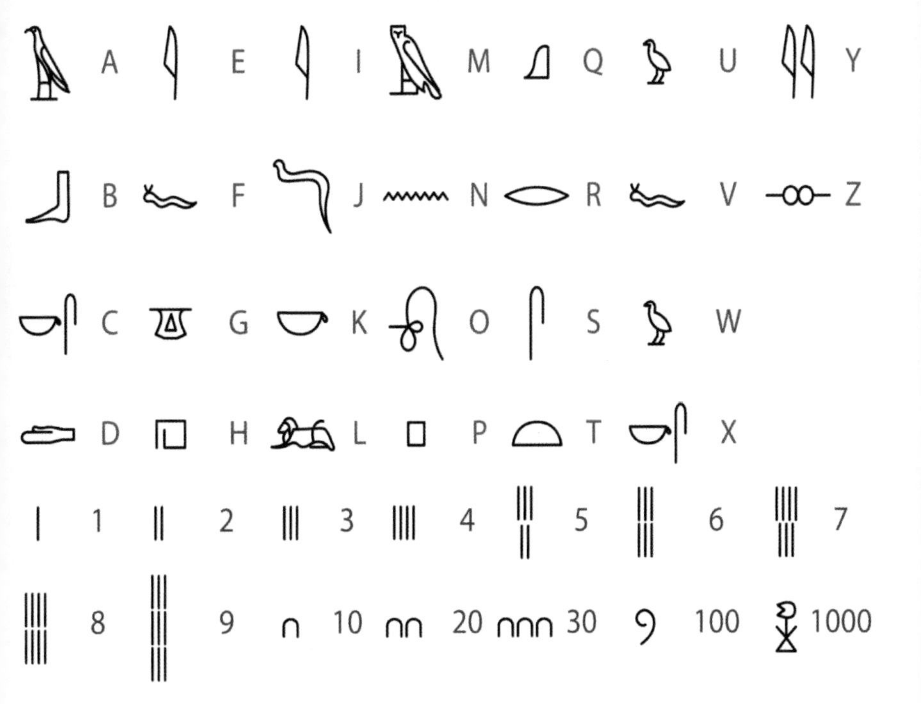

Printed in Great Britain
by Amazon

83915265R00042